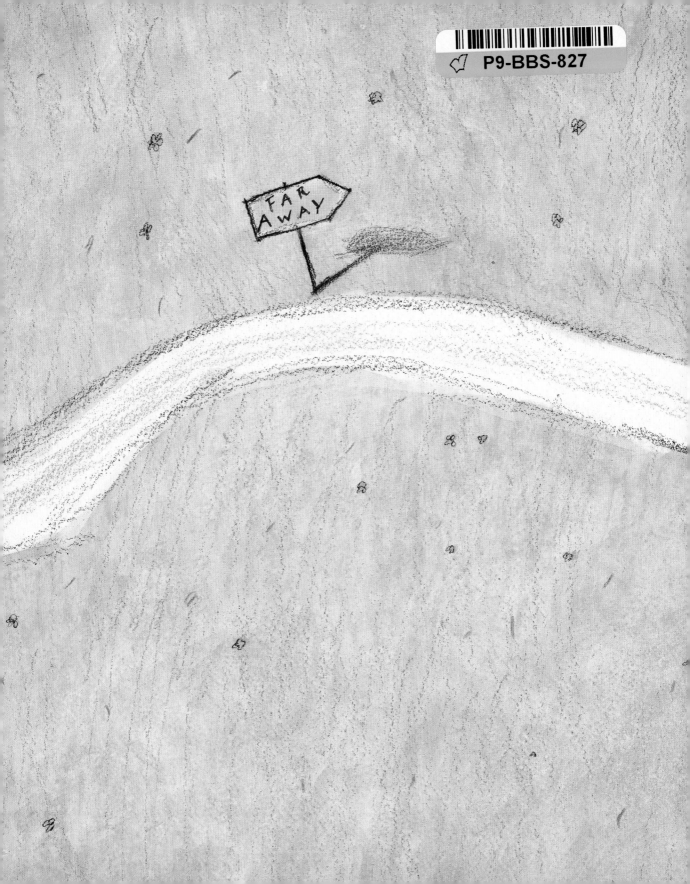

Three Little Bikers

by Tony Johnston

illustrated by G. Brian Karas

AN UMBRELLA BOOK

Alfred A. Knopf · New York

For bikers, little and big
—T. J.

For Leslie Falzone, a shining light
—G. B. K.

THIS IS AN UMBRELLA BOOK PUBLISHED BY ALFRED A. KNOPF, INC.

Text copyright © 1994 by Tony Johnston
Illustrations copyright © 1994 by G. Brian Karas

Library of Congress Cataloging-in-Publication Data

Johnston, Tony
Three little bikers / by Tony Johnston ; pictures by G. Brian Karas.
p.   cm. — (An Umbrella book)
Summary: Follows the adventures of three little bicyclists as they ride through the countryside.
ISBN 0-679-84701-4 (trade) — ISBN 0-679-94701-9 (lib. bdg.)
[1. Bicycles and bicycling—Fiction.] I. Karas, G. Brian, ill. II. Title. III. Series: Umbrella books.
PZ7.J6478th   1994
[E]—dc20   93-39249

Manufactured in the United States of America
10 9 8 7 6 5 4 3 2 1

Three little bikers took their bikes one day,
and they rode far away.

The grass was green. The trees were too.
And the sky was blue
as they rode
with their packs on their backs
and three little flags that went
flap, flap, flap
in the wind.

Wind blew in their hair.
It blew everywhere
and puffed their shirts
like little white sails.
And it tickled,
so they giggled
as they rode
with their packs on their backs
and three little flags that went
flap, flap, flap
in the wind.

They rode through gravel
ping, ping, ping.
They rode through dust.
Whissssssh!
They rode through grass
and left their tracks
like three quick little snakes.

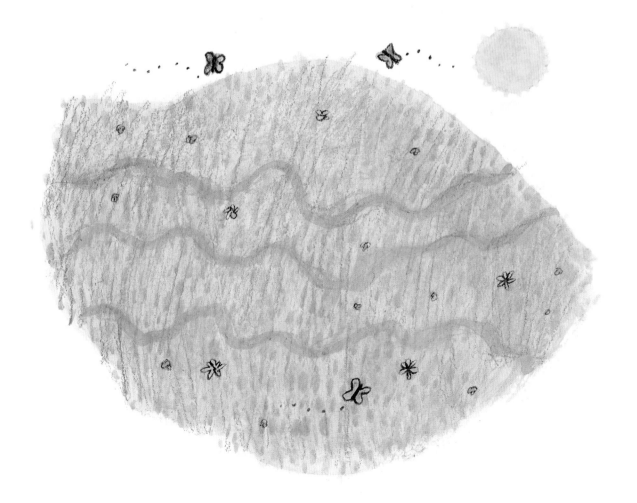

They came to a gully,
steep and deep.
Should they? Could they? Would they cross?
Yes! Yes! Yes!

They raced down the gully
and up again
with their packs on their backs
and three little flags that went
flap, flap, flap
in the wind.

They came to a puddle,
fat with rain.
Should they? Could they? Would they cross?
Yes! Yes! Yes!

Whooosh!
They splashed
a shiny silver spray.
Then they raced away.

They came to a hill,
green and high.
Should they? Would they? Could they climb?
Yes! Yes! Yes!

They crept up the hill
with their packs on their backs
and three little flags that went
flop, flop, flop.
Like three little turtles
hurrying up.

At the very top
they shouted, "Here we are!"
And a voice just like
a voice in a jar
shouted, "Are! Are! Are!"

A bird flew up.
So they flew too
and soared like birds
all over the hill
with their arms like wings that went
flap, flap, flap
in the wind.

They rolled all over
like rolling stones.
Grass stuck in their hair.
It stuck everywhere.
And it tickled,
so they giggled
as they rolled.

Then they flopped in the grass
and ate—*chomp, chomp, chomp*—
like three hungry little ants
till their lunch was gone.

They blew into their bags
and popped them—
Bang! Bang! Bang!

And they sang a loud song
like popping bags,

and they sang a soft song
like birds

till the day got old
and the sky got red
and they knew
it was time to leave.

They looked over the hill,
far, FAR, FAR.
Should they? Could they? Would they go?
Yes! Yes! Yes!

So—
three little bikers raced down again
with their packs on their backs
and three little flags that went
flap, flap, flap
in the wind.

As they rode
they sang a song.
And as night came on
their headlights glowed
like three little fireflies
all the way
home.

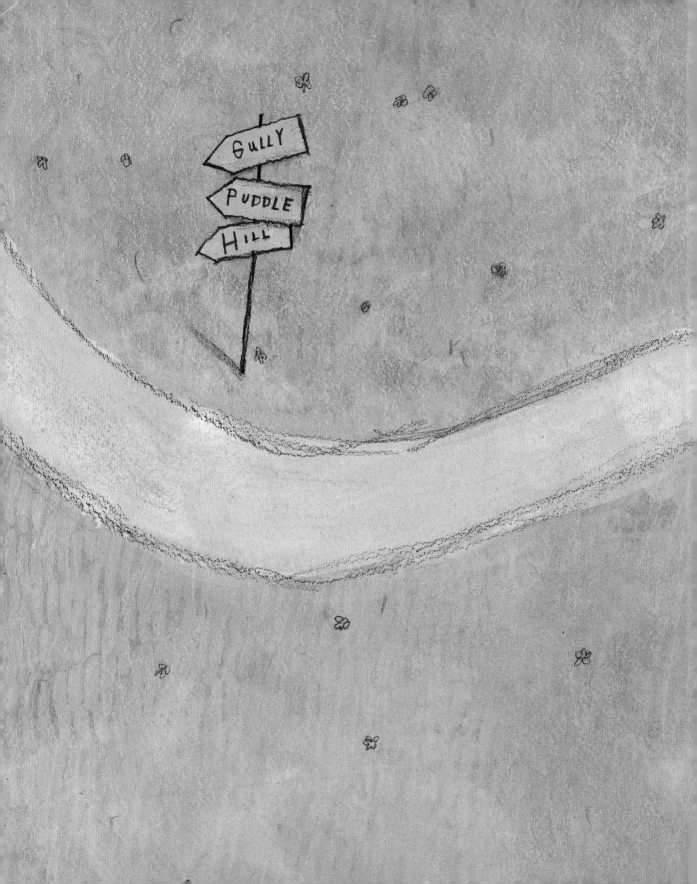